# NORSE MYTHS & LEGENDS

AS TOLD BY PHILIP ARDAGH

ILLUSTRATED BY STEPHEN MAY

Dillon Press

# MYTH OR LEGEND?

Long before people could read or write, stories were passed on by word of mouth. Every time they were told, they changed a little, with a new character added here and a twist to the plot there. From these ever-changing tales, myths and legends were born.

### WHAT IS A MYTH?

A myth is a traditional story that isn't based on something that really happened and is usually about superhuman beings. Myths are made up, but often explain local customs or natural phenomena—such as thunder.

### WHAT IS A LEGEND?

A legend is very like a myth. The difference is that a legend might be based on an event that really happened or a person who really existed. That's not to say that the story hasn't changed over the years.

### WHO WERE THE NORSE PEOPLE?

The Norse people, who told these stories around the fireside on cold winter nights, came from Norway, Sweden, Denmark,

Finland, and Iceland, though they did settle elsewhere. These were the Viking races—brave, warrior people living in tough times in a cruel climate—and most of their myths and legends were about brave warrior gods. The earliest versions were being told almost 2,000 years ago, but the stories have changed a great deal since then.

### HOW DO WE KNOW?

Many scenes from myths and legends appear on Viking carvings, and there are also two main written sources. These are called the *Poetic Edda* (or the *Elder Edda*) and the *Prose Edda*. The *Prose Edda* is a collection of the most famous myths and legends, written down by a man from Iceland called Snorri Sturluson, who lived from 1179 to 1241.

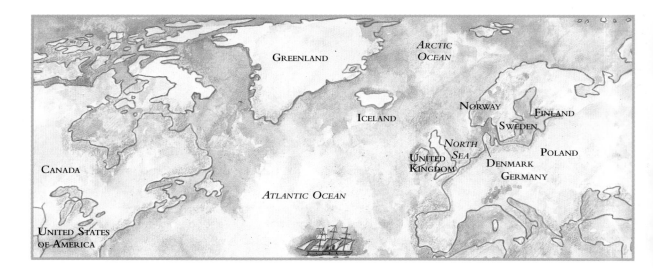

The stories were already very old when he put them on paper, but it's thanks to him that we know so much today. The *Poetic Edda* is made up of 34 poems by different people and was given this name when they were collected in the seventeenth century.

## THE NORSE WORLD

The Norse people had a very clear picture of what their world looked like. In fact, they saw it as nine different worlds.
ALFHEIM home of the light elves.
VANAHEIM home of the fertility gods.
ASGARD home of the warrior gods called the Aesir, connected by **Bifrost** (a rainbow bridge) to
MIDGARD home of the humans.
NIDAVELLIR land of the dwarfs.
JOTUNHEIM land of the giants.
SVARTALFHEIM home of the dark elves.
NIFLHEIM includes Hel, the realm of the dead.
MUSPELL a place of fire.

## THE TREE OF LIFE

The nine worlds were held together by the roots of the mighty **Yggdrasil,** a tree growing up into the stars. **Ratatosk,** a squirrel, ran up and down the branches, trunk, and roots of Yggdrasil, delivering insults between the birds and the dragon **Nidhogg**. The dragon chewed at the roots, trying to destroy the tree.

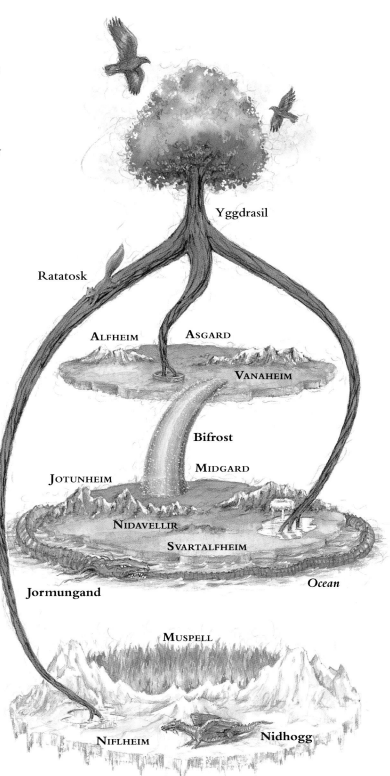

Yggdrasil

Ratatosk

ALFHEIM    ASGARD

VANAHEIM

Bifrost

MIDGARD

JOTUNHEIM

NIDAVELLIR

SVARTALFHEIM

*Ocean*

Jormungand

MUSPELL

NIFLHEIM    Nidhogg

# Gods, Giants, & Dwarfs

In some myths and legends, the gods are immortal and live forever. That's not so with the Norse gods. They *can* be killed. In fact, Norse myths and legends predict that one day all the gods *will* be killed in a mighty battle against the giants called Ragnarok. Here are some of the characters you will meet in this book. Many have more than one wife or husband. Some of the alternative spellings of their names are in parentheses.

ODIN (Woden)  One-eyed chief of all the gods, has a throne, Hlidskialf, and two advisers: the ravens Hugin and Munin. A brave warrior, he is the husband of Frigga and father of many of the gods.

FRIGGA (Frigg)  Wife of Odin and mother of most of his children. Her favorite son is the handsome Balder. She is the most powerful goddess in Asgard.

THOR  God of thunder. Rides across the skies in a chariot pulled by goats, has the hammer Mjollnir and the belt Meginjardir. Short tempered, but likes humans. A popular god with the Norse people.

TYR  God of war. The bravest of all the gods, as well as being honorable and true. Famous for having just one hand. If you want to know how he lost the other one, read "Tyr and the Jaws of Fenris" (page 19).

BALDER (Baldr)  God of light. The most handsome of all the gods, and Frigga's favorite son.

HODER (Hod, Hodr)  Balder's twin brother, who is blind. The prophecies say that after the mighty battle of Ragnarok he and Balder will be born again.

LOKI  Master trickster, half a giant and half a god, friend of Odin and Thor and murderer of Balder. Sometimes very funny, but can be very cruel.

HEL (Hela)  Goddess of death, daughter of Loki. The lower half of her body is like a corpse's, with exposed bones and putrid flesh.

FREY (Freyr)  God of summer, whose chariot is pulled by a huge wild boar.

FREYA (Freyja) Goddess of beauty, whose chariot is pulled by two large cats.

KVASIR Said to be the wisest of all the gods in Asgard.

HOENIR (Honir) In some stories about the earliest gods, he is said to be Odin's brother. In others, that honor goes to Ve and Vili.

AEGIR (Hler) God of the sea, husband of Ran. Lord of the world beneath the waves where drowned sailors spend their days.

RAN Goddess of the sea, who pulls sailors from their boats in a large net, dragging them under water.

HEIMDALL The god who guards Bifrost, the rainbow bridge joining the home of the gods to the other worlds.

UTGARD-LOKI The giant king of Utgard, in Jotunheim. Very clever and crafty. Once disguised himself as a giant called Skrymir to teach Thor a lesson.

HREIDMAR A dwarfish king with three sons—Otter, Fafnir, and Regin. Held Odin hostage for a huge pile of treasure.

FAFNIR A son of Hreidmar. Killed his father for his treasure, exiled his brother Regin, then turned himself into a dragon.

HYRROKKIN A terrifying giantess who rides an enormous wolf, using writhing vipers as reins.

SKIRNIR A brave and faithful servant to the god Frey.

*The Viking era was from about A.D. 700 to 1070. This is a Viking runestone. The carvings are called runes and are the earliest form of Norse writing.*

# THOR IN THE LAND OF THE GIANTS

A mighty war chariot hurtled across the
night sky pulled by two massive goats
with burning eyes and vicious, curled horns.
Their hoofs cracked the air around them with sparks
of lightning and filled the darkness with the sound
of thunder. At the reins stood a god with wild hair,
a wild beard, and wild eyes: a warrior god.
This was Thor, the god of thunder.

ONCE THOR VISITED a place called Utgard, in the land
of the giants. With him went his friend Loki, who was half
a giant and half a god, and two servant children, Thialfi and his
sister Roskva.

Around his waist Thor wore Meginjardir, a thick belt that
doubled his already superhuman strength. Tucked into it was his
gigantic throwing hammer called Mjollnir—a magic hammer that
always returned to him once it had struck and killed an enemy.
Even a glancing blow from it meant certain death.

When Thor and his band of travelers entered the vast hall of
the king of the giants, the giants laughed at him. They called him
"small" and "insignificant" and mocked him.

"Silence!" cried Thor, raising his bone-crushing hammer above
his head. "Even if I were a simple traveler, I would not expect to
be treated in this way. Where is your respect?"

"Respect?" bellowed Utgard-Loki, king of the giants, his voice
echoing around the massive hall.

"Respect has to be earned," he laughed. "If you or your followers can beat my giants at one simple challenge, then we shall respect you."

"Very well," replied Thor, his thin-lipped smile hidden by his beard. "We accept." He knew that he could defeat the giants at anything.

Thor's friend Loki pushed his way to the front of the group.

"I challenge anyone to beat me in an eating competition!" he cried. He felt sure that he would win because there was only one thing he enjoyed more than mischief-making, and that was eating.

"An excellent challenge!" boomed the giant king. "Let us prepare."

Soon a massive table was laid with plates of food from end to end. At one end stood Loki. At the other end was a strange-looking giant named Logi, dressed in flaming orange.

On a nod from the giant king, the race began. Both Loki and Logi ate as fast as they could, working their way down the table. When they met in the middle, Loki had eaten every scrap of meat, every vegetable, and every piece of fruit from his half of the table. Who could beat that?

The giant, Logi, that was who—for he had eaten all that and more. He had eaten every bone and even the plates on which the food was served. Thor's group had failed in their first task.

Next Thor's servant boy Thialfi agreed to a race against a boy giant called Hugi across the floor of the vast stone-flagged hall. Thialfi and Hugi lined up, and Thor threw back his head and shouted "GO!"

Thialfi sprang forward with all his might, only to hear the giants cheering as though someone had already reached the far wall. Someone had. To the boy's utter amazement, Hugi had already run the course and was being hoisted on the giants' shoulders in celebration.

Exhausted and defeated, Thialfi returned to his master.

"You did your best," bellowed Thor. "We only have to beat them at one task, and now it is my turn."

He faced the king of the giants, who was leaning back in his huge wooden throne, clearly enjoying events.

"What challenge will you make, little thunder god?" the king asked, a chuckle rising in his throat.

"I challenge you to a drinking match," said Thor, his eyes burning with anger at the way the giants were treating him. "We'll see who can drink the most horns of wine."

"Our wine is very strong," said the king. "Let us see who can drink the most horns of water." He clapped his enormous hands, and a huge drinking horn was brought into the hall. "You start," said the king.

Thor tipped the end of the horn to his lips and drank and drank and drank . . . but, however much he drank, he could never empty the horn. Finally he had to admit defeat.

"If you can't drain even a single horn, there's no competition," shrugged the giant king. "Perhaps you should try something easier, such as lifting my cat from its place by the fire and putting it on my lap."

Thor's face reddened with anger.

"Oh, well, if that's too difficult for you . . . ," the giant teased him.

Thor charged toward the fireplace and the sleeping cat.

"That's strange," Roskva whispered to her brother. "I'm sure that cat wasn't there a moment ago."

Thor reached the cat, bent down, and tried to lift it with one hand . . . then two hands . . . then with both arms. He couldn't lift so much as a single paw off the warm hearth.

Thor couldn't believe what was happening. He was a god, a hero. The people of Midgard stayed up late into the night telling stories of his incredible strength and amazing adventures. What was happening? Ever since he had set foot in Utgard, things had gone terribly wrong.

"I'm tired of your failures," sighed the king of the giants. "Where is the fun in the sport when our two sides are so unevenly matched?"

"Then I offer you one last challenge," said Thor, his deep voice almost a snarl. "I challenge any one of you to a wrestling match. It doesn't matter which of you, the strongest or the tallest—"

"Yes, yes, yes!" said the king with a dismissive wave. "I'll supply you with a worthy opponent. Elli?"

From behind the chief's chair came an old woman—not a giant, just an ordinary-looking old woman, with a bent back and wrinkled skin.

"Here is your wrestling partner, Thor," said the king.

"You expect me to wrestle against her?" gasped Thor.

"You talk of respect but show none," the giant responded with a flash of anger. "This is my old nursemaid. She brought me up as if I were her own son. She is worthy of anything."

"Very well," said Thor, stepping into the center of the hall with the old woman, circled by a ring of spectators.

"There's something wrong," whispered Roskva. "I'm sure that nothing is as it seems."

"Let the wrestling match begin!" cried Loki.

Despite her age Elli was extremely strong. At first Thor was clearly in control, wrestling her this way and that . . . but after much puffing and grunting, the old woman had him down on one knee.

"Enough!" the giant king yelled. "This is no contest. My old nursemaid wins!"

Thor felt humbled. Time and again he and his group had been beaten. He was ashamed. They hadn't won a single challenge and were not worthy of the respect of the giants. The king led them to the gates of his kingdom.

"Now you are leaving, I can tell you the truth of what happened," said the king. "The opponent Loki faced in the eating competition was really Fire, and nothing has a hunger like fire, which eats everything in its path." Loki gasped in amazement.

"As for Hugi, Thialfi's opponent in the race, he was no boy giant but Thought itself, and nothing is faster than a thought. Not even the world's fastest runner could have beaten him."

Thialfi's eyes opened wide in wonder.

"And as for the drinking horn, the other end was in the ocean, which was why you could never empty it," said the giant king. "But you drank so much, Thor, you created the coming in and the going out of the sea." Which is why we now have tides.

"What about the cat?" demanded Roskva.

"The harmless cat that Thor could not lift was Loki's son, Jormungand, magically transformed," the king confessed.

"He is the giant serpent who circles the whole earth, so it was not surprising that Thor couldn't lift him."

"And Elli, your old nursemaid?" asked Thor.

"Old Age herself," said the king, "and old age defeats us all in the end."

Thor felt a fool. "Why did you do this to us?" he asked, in a smaller, quieter voice than he had ever used before.

"Because on your way to Utgard—on the night you slept in a giant's discarded glove, believing it to be a stable—you showed disrespect to a sleeping giant, striking him with your hammer to stop his snoring," the king reminded him. "I was that giant, and I would be dead from the mighty blow of Mjollnir if I hadn't been protected by magic. Now leave my kingdom and never return."

So Thor left with Loki, Thialfi, and Roskva, proud at how well they had competed against Fire, Thought, the Ocean, Jormungand, and Old Age, but also knowing that he been taught a valuable lesson.

Thor went on to many victories and still travels in his chariot across the skies, creating storms wherever he goes. He is remembered and honored, and gives his name to Thursday, which means Thor's day . . . but now he has greater respect for the giants, who are ruled by a very wise and cunning king.

# THE CURSE OF ANDVARI'S RING

This is a story that spans many generations. It begins with three gods disguised as ordinary human beings, and with an otter that isn't an otter at all. It ends with a young hero and a dragon that was once a dwarf. What brings all these strange people and creatures together? A hoard of gold and a cursed ring.

ONE DAY ODIN, chief of the gods, and his brother Hoenir were walking along a riverbank with Loki. They stopped to watch an otter skillfully catch a salmon in the water.

"That animal is a fine hunter," said Hoenir, "and it has caught a fine fish."

"And made me realize just how hungry I am," said Odin.

"Then let the hunter become the hunted!" cried Loki, throwing a stone at the otter and killing it with a single blow. Odin made a fire, and while Hoenir cooked the huge salmon that had been trapped between its paws, Loki skinned the otter.

Just then a dwarf appeared. He was obviously angry about something because he was ranting and raving so much that none of them could understand a word he was saying. Then he started to gnash his teeth and jump up and down in an absolute fury.

"Calm down, little man," said Odin, putting a friendly hand on the dwarf's shoulder.

This seemed to make the dwarf even angrier.

"Little man?" he spluttered. "*Little man?* I am King Hreidmar!"

"Will you join us in our meal, your majesty?" asked Hoenir.

"I do not eat with murderers!" snapped the dwarfish king.

Loki leaped up, the knife he'd used to skin the otter glinting in the sunlight, but Odin held him back.

"Be careful who you call a murderer," said Odin quietly. "Do you know who I am?"

"You could be the chief of the gods for all I care," cried Hreidmar. "You are still murderers. I sent one of my sons to catch that fish for my dinner table. Like me, he's a shapeshifter. . . ."

". . . and he changed himself into an otter?" asked Hoenir, realizing with horror what had happened. Loki had killed and skinned a dwarfish prince!

Just then two other dwarfs appeared, brandishing weapons. These were Hreidmar's other two sons, Fafnir and Regin. Their weapons were magical and could do the gods serious harm.

"The three of you will be put to death for what you've done!" cried the king.

"Wait," said Odin. "Your son's death was a terrible mistake. Isn't there some way we can repay you for this dreadful accident?"

Hreidmar's eyes lit up at the mention of the word *repay*. He thought for a moment, then said: "I shall let you live if you can stuff the otter's skin with gold and then bury it upright in a pile of treasure, high enough to cover it from nose to tail!"

"We shall gladly do this," said Odin, and as he spoke, he noticed the otter's skin growing bigger and bigger and bigger. There was dwarfish magic in the air, and it would take an enormous amount of treasure to fulfill the bargain.

Leaving Odin and Hoenir as hostages, Loki went off in search of gold. Soon he reached a bend in the river and came upon a waterfall . . . and another dwarf. Loki recognized him as King Andvari, who was reputed to have a hoard of fabulous treasure hidden away somewhere.

As luck would have it, Andvari dived off the bank and turned into a beautiful gleaming trout before he hit the water.

As quick as a flash, Loki pulled out a net borrowed from the goddess Ran—the net she used to pull drowning sailors to their watery graves beneath the waves—and threw it into the water, catching the furious Andvari in its mesh.

"Let me out!" screamed Andvari, who'd already turned himself back into his usual dwarfish form.

No matter how hard he struggled, he couldn't free himself from the goddess's net. Finally he agreed to give Loki a sack of his gold in return for his freedom. The dwarf then took Loki to the place where his gold was hidden. There was so much of it that Loki and Andvari were both bathed in a golden light.

When Loki saw the dwarf's fabulous treasure, he wasn't satisfied with just a sackful. He wanted it all . . . every last piece, down to the ring around Andvari's arm.

"I wouldn't take that if I were you," said the dwarf.

"But you're not me . . . and I choose to have it!" grinned Loki.

"It will bring bad luck, I warn you," said Andvari, who was feeling very sick at the thought of losing all his gold. But Loki snatched the ring and kept it for himself—unaware that the cunning dwarf had laid a curse on it before passing it over.

Using all his strength and skill, Loki made his way back to Hreidmar with the treasure. Odin and Hoenir were pleased at Loki's return, but Hreidmar was happiest of all. Perhaps it was the sight of all that gold that made him smile from ear to ear.

Loki set about stuffing the huge otter's skin and burying it upright, from head to tail, in Andvari's gold.

Soon it was done, and Hreidmar was jumping up and down with glee in a most unkinglike manner.

He was just about to release Odin and Hoenir when he spotted something amiss.

"Wait!" he cried.

"What is it?" asked Loki, who was sure that he had kept his part of the bargain.

"The agreement was that you cover the whole otter with gold," said Hreidmar, a wicked smile spreading across his face.

"And I have," said Loki.

"Then what is this?" demanded the dwarfish king, pointing to the pile of treasure.

Loki peered closely at the pile and could just make out the tip of a single otter's whisker sticking out to one side.

"I have just the thing to cover that," he said, hurriedly placing Andvari's cursed ring over the whisker.

So Odin, Hoenir, and Loki were free to go and went on their way.

The story didn't end there, however, for King Hreidmar and his remaining sons. The curse of the ring was already weaving its evil magic. It started by working its way into Fafnir's mind, making him jealous of his father's new-found wealth.

Soon he wanted the gold for himself—so badly that, one night, he murdered Hreidmar while he lay sleeping.

"Now the gold is mine!" Fafnir whispered into the darkness. "I shall share it with no one."

Just then Regin appeared, yawning.

"What is it, brother?" he asked. Then he noticed his father lying dead at Fafnir's feet and a mad look in Fafnir's eye. He turned and fled, never to return to the land of the dwarfs.

With Regin gone, Fafnir still worried about the safety of his treasure. What if Loki came back, or someone else learned the whereabouts of these untold riches? He would have to guard the hoard forever. So Fafnir turned himself into a dragon and settled down on top of the huge pile of gold.

Time passed, and in exile among humans his brother Regin taught people many dwarfish tricks and ways of life. He showed people how to fashion metals to make tools and weapons, how to harness an ox to a plow, and how to build houses.

Regin had a son who grew to be a strong and handsome. His name was Sigurd. He learned the story of his evil uncle, Fafnir, who had caused his father to live away from his own kind, and traveled to the land of the dwarfs to track him down.

On his journey Sigurd met a stranger who gave him a very important piece of information. He told the young hero that Fafnir, in the form of a scaly dragon, sat day and night on top of his treasure and guarded it with such ferocity that no one could hope to get close enough to harm him. The only time the dragon left the treasure and dropped his guard was when he went to drink from the river.

With this important knowledge about the dragon, Sigurd dug himself a trench near the river and crouched out of sight in it. When Fafnir, in his dragon form, grew thirsty, he slithered off the golden hoard and made his way down to the water—his scaly body passing over the trench where Sigurd waited.

Sigurd grasped his sword and with all his strength plunged the blade into his wicked uncle's breast, tearing it open and killing him.

**The exile of Sigurd's father and the death of his grandfather, King Hreidmar, had been avenged . . . and the curse of Andvari's ring had claimed yet another victim.**

# TYR AND THE JAWS OF FENRIS

A long, long time ago, before most of these tales were even in the minds of those who could see far into the future, the mischievous Loki—half a god and half a giant—secretly married the terrifying giantess Angurboda. They had three children: a writhing serpent, a hideous goddess who was half living, half corpse, and a huge wolf.

L OKI TRIED TO keep his three children a secret, hiding them away. He was well aware that Odin, the one-eyed chief of all the gods, could see everything from his throne.

What Odin saw troubled him greatly. He was horrified by Loki's brood and how big and powerful each was becoming. It seemed likely that they would grow up to be a threat to the gods themselves.

Odin tracked down Loki and his children to a cave, burst in, and grabbed the serpent, spinning it around his head until it flew from his grasp and landed in the ocean. There it grew large enough to circle the whole earth and bite its own tail. This was Jormungand, the giant serpent who lives there still.

As for the hideous rotting goddess, Odin threw her down into Niflheim where she became ruler of the dead and that place that now bears her name—Hel. Here she feeds off the bones of those who do not die honorably in battle.

This left the third child, the wolf called Fenris.

Odin hoped that if he treated Fenris with kindness and respect, he might grow up to be loyal to the gods.

He took Fenris back to Asgard, where he was troubled to find that most of his fellow gods and goddesses were already more than a little afraid of the beast, although he was still a cub.

There was only one god who didn't seem at all frightened of this massive wolf, and that was Tyr, the god of war. It was he who fed Fenris daily. He knew no fear and was kind to the extraordinary creature.

As the wolf grew larger and larger, Odin called a council of gods and goddesses to decide what should be done.

"According to the prophecies, this will be the creature that destroys you, Odin," said one. "I say we kill him before this can happen."

"Prophecies cannot be altered," another protested.

"We cannot slay Fenris, for it was you who brought him here to Asgard and that would be wrong," said Tyr to Odin.

"I agree," said the chief of all the gods. "So what is to be done?"

They finally decided that Fenris needed to be held in place with a large chain so that he couldn't roam free and do any harm. No ordinary chain would do, so they found one famous for its strength, called Laeding.

The problem was how to bind Fenris with it. He would never allow them simply to tie him up. So they suggested to the wolf that this was a game.

"You know we're proud of how strong we are," said one of the gods. "Here's a chance for you to show off your strength. We will bind you in this chain and see how long it takes you to break free."

Unaware that this was a special chain, Fenris agreed and was bound up in Laeding. In next to no time, the enormous wolf was free. He simply tensed his muscles and burst every link of the chain —a shower of twisted pieces of metal fell to the ground.

Pretending to be delighted at how he had proved his incredible strength, the gods praised Fenris, then slunk off, muttering to one another at their failure.

Next they came back with an even stronger chain, known as Dromi, and they used the same trick as before to tie up Fenris.

It seemed only a moment before the chain burst and the huge wolf was free once more.

It was then that the gods realized something that should have occurred to them from the very beginning. Only the most extraordinary binding would be able to hold Fenris. This beast was the son of a giantess and of Loki, who was half a god and also half a giant.

Odin sent for Skirnir, the faithful servant of Frey, god of summer.

"I need you to go quickly to the land of the dwarfs and to visit the underground caves of the finest craftsmen," he said. "Ask them to make the strongest rope or chain, bound together with the strongest magic."

"And what do I offer them in return, sir?" asked the servant, only too well aware of the importance of his visit to the land of the dwarfs, and of the dwarfs' love of gold.

"Tell them that it is to bind Fenris, and they'll accept no payment. They'll know how vital this is to me," said Odin, his single eye fixed firmly on Skirnir. "Do you understand?"

"I understand," nodded Skirnir, and he was off.

Once Skirnir reached the land of the dwarfs, he asked their finest craftsman to create a magical rope that no one—however strong —would be able to break.

"To do this, I need the strongest magic, including five most special ingredients," said the dwarf, whose name is a secret to this day. "I need the sound of the cat's footfall, the beards of women, the mountain's root, the fish's voice, and the bird's spittle."

Now those of you who are thinking that cats' footfalls are silent, that women don't have beards, that mountains don't have roots, and neither do fish have voices, nor birds have spittle are right.

It was because the dwarfs took all these ingredients away from the world of humans long, long ago to fashion the rope Gleipnir, that not one of these things exists any more.

When Skirnir returned to Asgard with the rope, some of the gods were unimpressed. Gleipnir was as smooth and soft as a ribbon made of silk. How could this hold Fenris?

But Odin trusted the magic and took it to the wolf.

"Let us bind you a third time and see if you can escape," he said. Fenris eyed the ribbonlike rope with suspicion.

"No," he said, at last.

"No?" gasped Odin. "Why not?"

"Because if it is an ordinary rope, as it appears, there's no pride in my being able to break free from it," said Fenris.

"If, on the other hand, it is a magic rope, woven from trickery, then I may not be able to escape from it . . . and why should I willingly walk into such a trap?"

Now Odin wasn't going to lie and deny that this was a trap, for that was exactly what it was intended to be.

"Listen," he said. "If you can't break free from this simple ribbonlike rope, you'll pose no threat to us, so of course we shall set you free."

"That may be true," said Fenris, "but I notice that you are careful not to say *when* you'll set me free."

He went on: "I shall play this game, but with one rule of my own. Let one of you put his hand in my mouth while I am tied up with this rope. That way we'll both prove each other's trust. I will trust you not to use trickery and to set me free if I fail. You will trust me not to bite unless . . ." Fenris paused, and ran his drooling tongue across his dagger-sharp teeth, ". . . unless you betray me."

There was silence. Odin looked from one god to another to another, waiting for one to take up the challenge.

Tyr stepped forward while the others looked on, some clutching the remains of the far-thicker chains from which Fenris had so easily freed himself. He thrust his hand between the jaws of the animal he had looked after since the day he had arrived as a pup in Asgard.

Then the gods tied Fenris in the ribbonlike bonds of the magical Gleipnir.

The harder the huge wolf struggled to free himself, the tighter the bonds became, until he could barely move at all.

Perhaps it was because he was tensing his jaw muscles when trying to use every ounce of his strength to free himself, or perhaps it was because he felt betrayed by the one god who had shown him kindness; either way, Fenris snapped his jaws shut, biting off Tyr's hand.

The wolf then opened his mouth wide and howled with such rage that one of the gods thrust a sword between his jaws to wedge them open.

And that is how Fenris came to be tied in place, his jaws wedged open wide. From his mouth poured saliva, which became the foaming torrents of a river. There the tormented animal will remain until the final battle of Ragnarok at the end of time, when he will be able to take revenge on those who trapped him.

And that is also how Tyr, the god of war, comes to have one hand. Some say that this is a sign that a true warrior can take only one side in battle. Some say it is sign that a sword only needs one blade. But many believe that it is a mark that Tyr proved himself to be a brave and loyal god who helped the other gods in a difficult task but was also true to Fenris, one of the three dreadful children of the mischievous Loki.

# THE GOD WHO
# LOVED A GIANTESS

Odin, the chief of all the gods, has a
magnificent throne carved from one
giant tree. So important and powerful is this
seat that it has a special name, Hlidskialf,
and only Odin and his wife may sit on it.
From this magical throne they see everything
that happens in all the nine worlds. . . .

ONE DAY Frey, the god of summer, found the throne empty.
Odin was away on one of his fantastic adventures, and there
were no other gods about. Frey couldn't resist climbing up onto
Hlidskialf's seat . . . just to see what it was like to sit there.

No sooner had Frey sat down than his eyes fell on a beautiful
light pulsating in the distance. It hypnotized him. Then the light
took on another form, with arms and legs and flowing hair of
such radiant beauty that Frey was stunned. This was the magical
figure of Gerda, a frost giantess. Frey fell instantly in love.

Now nothing else mattered to Frey. He couldn't sleep or eat.
All he could think about was the frost giantess.

But how could he make her love him in return?

He didn't dare tell the other gods what he was feeling because
then they'd know that he had sat on Odin's throne. But his
faithful servant Skirnir soon discovered his secret.

"I want you to travel to the land of the giants and convince
Gerda that I love her and want to marry her," said Frey.

Skirnir was well aware of the dangers of his quest and how unlikely he was to succeed. In return, he asked to be given Frey's magic sword, which could fly through the air and attack an enemy the moment it was drawn from its scabbard. He also borrowed Frey's magnificent horse, Blodughofi, who was afraid of nothing.

Frey gave them willingly. He also handed Skirnir 11 golden apples that would keep Gerda young forever if she ate them. Then he gave him an arm ring to present to the giantess. But this was no ordinary ring—it was Draupnir, Odin's magic ring. Skirnir didn't dare ask how Frey came to have it.

So Skirnir began his quest. It took him a day and a night to ride to the land of the giants, through forests and mountains. He stopped only once, to pick up a magical wooden staff he had found lying in his path.

At his journey's end an enormous hall loomed before him, surrounded by the red flames of an enchantress, protecting it from unwelcome visitors. On either side of the entrance were the biggest and most ferocious hounds Skirnir had ever seen.

But Frey's horse was not afraid of the flames or of the dogs and carried Skirnir past them into the palace. He told the giantess of his quest and of Frey's love for her.

She was unimpressed by the proposal of marriage.

Skirnir offered her the magic golden apples.

"Why should I wish to stay young forever, while those I love grow old around me?" she asked.

He offered her the arm ring of the chief of all the gods himself.

"What use is that to me?" she asked. "Odin may be mighty to gods and humans, but he'd make a very small giant. How could I hope to fit such a ring on even my smallest finger?"

Skirnir did not give up easily. He pointed to Frey's sword.

"This is Frey's magic sword," he said. "If I pull it from its scabbard, it will fly up to your neck and chop off your head."

Gerda laughed. "What good will that do? Frey will still be without a bride, and my father will rip you to pieces, starting with your arms."

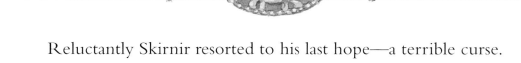

Reluctantly Skirnir resorted to his last hope—a terrible curse. He pulled out the wooden staff he had found on his journey there.

"If you will not marry Frey, I shall lay a curse on you," he shouted, his voice echoing around the vast room. "A curse that will make you hungry all the time, but make everything you eat taste like salt . . . a curse that will leave you standing by the entrance to the world of the dead, watching others in torment . . . a curse that will make you an ugly hag. . . ."

"Enough!" cried Gerda. "This Frey you talk of must want to marry me badly. Tell him that I shall be his wife," she sighed. "I will come to him after nine days and nights. Now, go."

Skirnir returned to Frey in triumph.

"What news?" cried the god of summer, stumbling forward to meet him, with a heavy heart and a sense of almost certain failure —for he could see that his servant was traveling alone.

"Gerda has agreed to be your bride," said Skirnir, "but you must wait nine days and nine nights until she comes to you."

Though delighted by Skirnir's news, the next nine days and nights were a torment to Frey. They were like the nine months of winter— cold and dark and seemingly never-ending.

Then, at last, the day came when Gerda left the great hall of her father, Gymir, and went to Frey, meeting him for the very first time . . . and the impossible happened. When the frost giantess stared into the eyes of the love-sick god, she, in turn, fell in love with him.

"Frey," she said, her voice cracking like a hard frost underfoot, "I forgive you your bribes and threats. Let us be together always."

**And they still are together, and will be until Ragnarok, the final battle at the end of time. Gerda's magical beauty can be seen today in the aurora borealis, or northern lights, which are strange, moving lights in the skies above the North Pole.**

# THOR'S STOLEN HAMMER

Only someone very foolish or very brave would dare to steal Thor's hammer, Mjollnir, but that's exactly what happened. The story of how Thor and Loki got it back is very funny in places, but the ending is no laughing matter.

ONE MORNING Thor woke up with a terrible headache and sat up, rubbing his eyes. He knew that something was wrong before he reached for his magic hammer in his belt, and found it missing. He had sensed that Mjollnir wasn't at his side.

Roaring with rage, he called to his friend Loki, who was asleep by the fire. If anyone had taken Mjollnir as a foolish prank, it would be Loki. But Loki protested that he knew nothing about the whereabouts of the hammer. So where had it gone?

Thor paced up and down the hall, the sound of his footsteps thundering through the skies. When he was angry, the people of Midgard soon knew about it as bolts of lightning crashed around their ears.

"Perhaps you dropped it somewhere?" Loki suggested.

"WHAT?" roared Thor.

"It was only a suggestion," said Loki, but he had to admit that it was a foolish one. There was probably only one thing Thor loved more than his hammer and that was his wife, the goddess Sif.

"Someone has stolen it!" cried Thor, his face so red with anger that it almost matched his beard. "You must help me find it!"

Loki didn't wait to be asked twice. When Thor was angry, it was best to do as he suggested.

Loki decided that he needed to find the quickest way of searching for Mjollnir. One way would be to sit on Odin's throne and see the whole world at once, but he wasn't so foolish as to risk that.

Then he thought of asking to borrow Frey's amazing longboat, which could travel through the skies. It was large enough to hold all the gods and goddesses at once, but when folded up was small enough fit in your pocket. Loki decided against this because the thief might see the shadow the longboat cast on the ground below and hide Mjollnir.

Loki needed a quick way of traveling across the nine worlds without being recognized or attracting attention. Then he had an excellent idea. He approached Freya, the goddess of beauty. She had a giant falcon's coat, which she often wore to fly around in disguise. This was just what Loki needed and—because of the importance of his task—Freya agreed to lend it to him.

After a while Loki heard stories in the wind that a giant called Thrym had stolen Mjollnir and buried it deep in the earth where no one would find it. Loki asked around and discovered that Thrym was no warrior giant, but a rather ordinary fellow who was head over heels in love with Freya. In fact, Thrym would only reveal Mjollnir's hiding place if the beautiful goddess agreed to marry him.

When Loki told Thor what he had discovered, Thor was delighted. The solution was simple: Freya must become Thrym's bride so that he could have his trusty weapon back. Thor and Loki went to Freya.

"You know how important Mjollnir is—not only to me, but also to all the gods," Thor reminded her. "This mighty weapon has protected the honor of Asgard on many an occasion."

"I am aware of that," Freya nodded, with a suspicious expression on her beautiful face, for she knew that Thor was leading up to something. "That was why I was willing to lend your mischievous friend my magic falcon's coat. Do you think I would have lent it otherwise?"

"Indeed not," said Thor, solemnly.

"I'm happy to report that we now know who has my hammer and why," he went on. "It is a giant called Thrym—"

"Who is a nice enough fellow, as giants go," Loki added, eyeing the necklace around the goddess of beauty's neck. He had once tried to steal it, but had failed.

"A splendid fellow, in fact," Thor agreed. "As a giant of wisdom and one who appreciates great beauty, Thrym wishes to marry you, Freya."

"Which we both think is an excellent idea," Loki added helpfully.

Freya looked from Thor to Loki, then back to Thor.

"You wish me to marry the giant who has stolen Mjollnir?" she asked. Thor nodded.

"And if I marry him, he'll give you back the hammer?" she went on. Thor nodded again.

"So it doesn't matter to you if this Thrym is a dragon, the ugliest of dwarfs, or a sniveling coward. What matters to you is that if I marry him, you'll have your precious hammer back?"

"Well . . . ," began Thor.

"Well . . . ," spluttered Loki.

Freya exploded with rage. She was so angry that even Thor, the great god of thunder himself, was shaken to his bones by her fury. Thor thanked Freya for the use of the falcon's coat; then he and Loki left the goddess with greater haste than their pride would have liked.

Thor and Loki decided that they'd have to trick Thrym into giving Thor his hammer back. But the question was how.

It was Heimdall who came up with the solution. Heimdall was the god whose duty it was to guard Bifrost, the rainbow bridge that connects Asgard, the land of the gods, to the other worlds.

Now Heimdall and Thor didn't see each other often because Thor wasn't allowed to cross the Bifrost. His footsteps were too thunderous and his goat-pulled chariot too wild to cross the rainbow without damaging it. He had to come and go by a different route.

Loki and Heimdall, on the other hand, knew each other only too well. It was Heimdall who had caught Loki trying to steal Freya's necklace, and the two were still enemies. The prophecies said that in the battle at the end of the world, Loki and Heimdall would kill each other.

Heimdall suggested that Thor should dress up as Freya and that Loki should dress as a handmaiden, a woman servant, traveling with her. Thor grumbled into his beard at the idea but, when he couldn't come up with a better one of his own, finally agreed to try it. In their unlikely disguises Thor and Loki went to visit Thrym in his giant hall.

There must have been strong magic at work that night, for despite his booming voice, his hard muscles, and red beard, Thor was mistaken for the beautiful Freya by the giant Thrym—who was so delighted when she arrived that he held a wedding banquet to celebrate.

At the banquet Thrym was shocked by the appetite of his wife-to-be. Thor forgot that he was supposed to be a goddess. He ate a whole ox and a huge platter of salmon and drank two barrels of ale.

Loki had to act fast before their host became suspicious. He quickly explained that Freya had been so excited about meeting and marrying Thrym that she hadn't been able to eat a thing for days.

"Now that you are together at last, she's making up for it," he added.

But things soon turned from bad to worse. Thrym tried to kiss Thor. Not surprisingly, Thor gave him a terrible glare.

"What have I done to offend you, my beautiful one?" Thrym asked. For a moment he suspected that things were not quite as they should be.

Thor was so busy trying to keep himself from tearing Thrym to pieces before he'd revealed where he'd hidden the hammer, that he was speechless.

Once again quick-witted Loki had to come to the rescue.

"No doubt you've noticed that burning look in my mistress's eyes," he said. Thrym nodded.

"Well, that is a look few men or giants ever live to see. That is the look of a goddess truly in love and burning with passion . . . ," Loki added quickly. "Freya is simply thrilled to be so near you."

Loki's words had the desired effect. Delighted by what he'd heard, Thrym got to his feet and called for silence.

"Giants and giantesses," he said grandly, "I am the happiest being in the nine worlds on this day. I love this goddess, Freya." He nodded his huge head in the direction of Thor, who was biting his tongue to keep himself from saying anything. "And she, in her turn, loves me."

The wedding party cheered, and it was then that Thrym made his mistake. . . . He produced Thor's hammer from its hiding place to impress his future bride. Before the giant knew what was happening, he felt Mjollnir snatched from his grasp by the "goddess" who had been his bride-to-be only moments before. But this was no goddess! How could he have been so blind?

Thrym stared in horror at the flaming red beard, the huge muscular body, and the eyes burning with rage. It was Thor himself!

This must have been the thieving giant's last thought before Thor brought his mighty hammer down on Thrym's head with a skull-crushing crunch. Then Loki and Thor turned on the other guests and killed every giant in the hall.

**Since then Mjollnir has stayed in the hands of Thor, its rightful owner, to be used to defend the honor of the gods and to strike whenever Thor's raging temper gets the better of him.**

# THE TRICK THAT KILLED A GOD

Balder was the most handsome of the gods. His hair gleamed like sunlight, and he brought goodness, happiness, and wisdom wherever he went . . . until he began to suffer from nightmares and the fear of death.

ODIN AND FRIGGA had many children, but Balder was Frigga's favorite. Balder had a twin brother called Hoder, who was blind, and, sadly, Frigga loved him least of all.

When Frigga learned of Balder's nightmares and fears of death, she decided to do all she could to protect him from harm. She went around the world making every animal, plant, stone, body of water, and illness promise not to harm Balder.

She spoke to the birds in the air, the insects, the leaves on the trees . . . and such was her power as the wife of the mighty Odin that they all promised not to so much as scratch her favorite son.

All, that is, except for one sprig of mistletoe that Frigga passed on her way home. Exhausted after her travels, Frigga glanced at the tiny plant and wondered what harm a small sprig of mistletoe could do to a god. Deciding that the answer was none at all, she did not stop to extract a promise from it.

The news soon spread that Balder was indestructible—that nothing would bruise or scratch him, let alone kill him. And it soon became a regular pastime for the other gods of Asgard to throw things at him in the place called Gladsheim.

Instead of careering through the skies, or hunting, or warring with the giants, the gods gathered to hurl anything and everything at Balder. Axes, arrows, knives, and rocks—every missile bounced off him.

The gods chose to do this at Gladsheim because it was a place of peace. This showed that the weapons were thrown in jest, not seriousness. Soon Balder was even more popular, and he stopped having nightmares.

Every time a missile was thrown and bounced off him, Balder tossed back his head and laughed at the shared fun of it all.

Once Thor came to Gladshiem with an enormous rock that was so large he barely had the strength to lift it—and he is the strongest god of all. He stepped forward and, with a cry, dropped the rock on Balder's head.

It should have squashed him flat. Instead the rock kept the promise it had made to Frigga and simply rolled off him and fell to the ground with a terrifying crash. Thor threw back his head and joined in Balder's laughter. This was great sport indeed!

Now, if it were possible, Balder looked even more handsome than he had before.

Thor's mischievous friend Loki did not share in the fun. He was used to being the center of attention and was jealous of Balder . . . so he plotted Balder's downfall.

"But how can I fight someone who is indestructible?" he asked himself thoughtfully.

If anyone knew the answer to that, it would be Frigga.

Loki disguised himself as an old woman and went to visit the goddess. Frigga didn't see through Loki's trickery and welcomed him.

When Loki asked about Balder and how nothing seemed to injure him, Frigga was happy to talk about her favorite son. She told the stranger how she had traveled to all corners of the world to extract the promise that nothing would harm him.

As the day wore on, Frigga became more and more talkative.
Soon the disguised Loki learned what he needed to know. Frigga
let slip that a single sprig of mistletoe growing to the west of Valhalla
hadn't promised anything, which meant that there was something
that might—possibly—be able to harm Balder.

"But how could a sprig of mistletoe do that?" she laughed.

"How indeed?" said Loki.

Loki went in search of the sprig of mistletoe. When he found
it, he realized that it must have grown since Frigga had seen it.
It was now long enough to make a useful weapon.

Loki quickly stripped off the berries and leaves and was left with a
thin, straight stem, which he sharpened to a point. He then returned to
the gods, who were having a great time throwing things at Balder. They
never tired of it. It was such fun watching even the heaviest of rocks
or the sharpest of axes bounce off him. What could they throw next?

That day Thor threw his mighty hammer, Mjollnir, at Balder. This
was a weapon feared by all. No one hit by it had survived. There were
tales of a sleeping giant called Skrymir once being struck with Mjollnir
and thinking that the gentle taps were no more than falling leaves—
but magic had been at work. Skrymir was, in reality, the giant king
Utgard-Loki, and the dents intended for his head were deep enough
to create valleys in the invisible hills that stood between his head and
the hammer's blows.

Mjollnir simply bounced off Balder and fell to the ground, and the
audience of gods cheered and joined in the laughter. Among them sat
Balder's blind twin brother, Hoder. Although he could enjoy the
conversation and laughter of the other gods, he couldn't join in the
fun because he couldn't watch everything bounce off his brother.
Loki pushed his way through the throng of gods and handed the
seated Hoder the pointed stick of mistletoe.

"Here, Hoder," he said. "You may not be able to see the result, but
you can at least take a shot like everyone else. Use my arm to guide
you, and you can throw this stick at Balder."

"Thank you, Loki," said Hoder.

Thinking he was simply taking part in the harmless game, Hoder let Loki guide his arm. Hoder threw the mistletoe arrow.

Because the mistletoe had not given the promise made by every other thing in the worlds, the arrow didn't bounce off Balder. The pointed tip tore through his clothes, pierced his heart, and killed him.

There was a shocked silence, followed by the thud of objects being dropped to the ground.

"Did you just throw that arrow at your twin?" one of the gods asked.

"Yes, I did!" said Hoder with a cheerful smile on his face. He was unaware of the terrible thing that had happened. "I'm sure Balder wasn't expecting that."

"So you don't deny it?" asked Balder's wife, the goddess Nanna.

"Of course not," said Hoder. "I threw it. . . ." Then he realized that there had been great distress in Nanna's voice. "Why? What's the matter?"

"The matter is that Balder is dead, and the arrow that killed him was thrown by you," said Thor sadly.

Horrified, Hoder explained what had happened. "I wanted to join in . . . and Loki gave me the arrow and helped me to aim, that's all. I didn't mean. . . ." His voice trailed off into silence.

At the mention of his name, a group of gods grabbed Loki, who was quietly trying to leave the scene of his dreadful crime.

"Friend or no friend, I should kill you where you stand, Loki," said Thor, blocking his path. "But Gladsheim is a place of peace, so there'll be no more killing here today."

The gods loosened their grip on Loki, who pulled himself free. He knew that he had gone too far and that there was no going back. None of the gods would forgive him for what he had done.

Loki turned and left Gladsheim for the last time, knowing that life would never be the same again.

While Nanna wept over the body of her dead husband, the mistletoe arrow still piercing his heart, the other gods hung their heads in sadness, for the law was clear.

Although they knew that Hoder had been tricked by Loki, it was Hoder's hand that had thrown the weapon that had killed the god of sunshine and happiness. By the law of the gods, this meant that Hoder would have to be punished, and the punishment was death.

Death did come to Hoder. Some time later Odin had another child, Vali. The mother of this boy was Rind, a cold goddess of the frozen earth. According to the prophecy, Vali would avenge Balder's death.

From the moment he was born, Vali began to grow before his mother's eyes. She and her nursemaid looked on in horror as the helpless baby grew into a fierce warrior in a matter of minutes. This was the man whose one mission in life was to fulfill the prophecy.

On the night he was born, Vali went to Asgard, the home of his father. There he killed his half brother Hoder, who had been tricked by Loki into killing his own twin brother. And the weapon Vali used? A single arrow. Some say that it was made from a stem of mistletoe.

**But what of Loki? For those of you who think he escaped lightly while the innocent Balder died, or those of you who wonder what Frigga did on hearing of the death of her favorite child, be patient, for there is more to come. . . .**

# BALDER'S FATE & LOKI'S DOWNFALL

Balder's body lay on the huge longboat, Ringhorn, and his fine possessions were laid out around him for the journey to the next life. At the edge of the water stood the gods, with Odin at the head, his two ravens, Hugin and Munin, on his shoulders, and his blue cloak billowing in the breeze.

Next to Odin stood his Valkyries, the beautiful women who took warriors who die in battle to the glorious place called Valhalla. Because he had died through Loki's trickery, Balder was denied a magnificent afterlife. He would begin his next life in Hel, where those who die of disease, accident, or old age go —a place without honor.

Thor paced up and down the shore, uneasy about the rows of giants who stood nearby as a mark of respect for the dead god. Among these giants were King Utgard-Loki, who had tricked Thor in the past, and Frey's wife, Gerda.

Odin stepped forward, removed his magic ring, Draupnir, from his arm and placed it in the ship. On that day it gained a new power: every ninth night it shed eight gold tears for the loss of Odin's favorite son, which became eight gold rings, each the size and weight of the original.

Then the giantess Hyrrokkin arrived on the back of an enormous wolf, using a pair of writhing vipers as reins. As she climbed off her mount, she asked someone to hold it.

Four warriors in bearskin shirts rushed forward. These were berserks, fearless and brutal fighters who attacked one another or rocks and trees if there was nothing else to fight.

But they couldn't control Hyrrokkin's wolf, so she had to calm him.

The giantess pushed Ringhorn down into the water. The funeral ship was so heavy and the splash so loud that it was heard in all nine worlds, including Niflheim. There Hel, Loki's hideous daughter, heard the sound and realized that Balder—killed by her father's trickery— was on his way to her.

Before the vessel drifted into the twilight, Thor stepped aboard. He held up his hammer to the sky and shouted the words that made sure that Balder's journey would be a safe one.

Then he brought the hammer down and touched it to the funeral pyre of dry wood on which the body lay. There was a shower of sparks. Flames began to lick at the dead body and soon became a sheet of roaring orange. On this, the saddest day in the history of Asgard, Balder's wife, Nanna, was overcome with grief and died. Her body was added to the pyre.

Even as Balder's corpse headed for Hel, the goddess Frigga hoped that she might be able to save her favorite son. She had asked for a volunteer to journey to Niflheim and beg the dreadful Hel to grant the one wish that only she could: to return Balder to the land of the living.

It was Hermod, messenger of the gods, who accepted this task. To speed his journey, he rode Odin's eight-legged horse, Sleipnir. He had to cross Gioll, the River of the Dead, over a bridge called Giollar—a bridge that, until that moment, had never been used by anyone living.

On the other side Hermod reached the entrance to Niflheim, where he was stopped by the hideous gatekeeper, Modgurd.

"Yesterday a whole army of dead rode over that bridge, and they didn't make as much noise as you!" she said. "Which suggests that you are very much alive and have no business here. What do you want?"

"I have come to speak to Hel," he explained. "To plead with her to return Balder and Nanna to the land of the living."

"Then you must hurry," said Modgurd. "They are already with Hel."

Hermod rode on at full speed and reached Hel's vast dining hall where he found Balder and Nanna. They were seated at a huge table.

"All over the nine worlds, everyone is grieving over the death of Balder," he told Hel. "He was loved by all. Isn't it right that you should give him back his life?"

"I am not so sure that the worlds grieve quite as much as you claim," said Hel, her rotting body hidden beneath her cloak. "If you can make everything, everywhere, living or dead, weep for the death of Balder, then I will let them both go. Otherwise they stay."

That was the message Hermod took back to Asgard, along with Odin's ring, Draupnir, which his dead son wanted returned to him. On hearing the news, Frigga sent messages to all corners of the worlds to tell all things that they must grieve the loss of her favorite child.

Soon the sound of sobbing filled the air. The grass wept dew. The rocks wept stalactites. The snow wept icicles. Tears of sap poured down the trunks of the trees.

Even Hel shed a tear in the knowledge that her father had caused Balder's death and would suffer for it. Everyone cried.

Everyone, that is, except for a giantess called Thok. When one of Frigga's messengers found her and told her of his mission, she said: "The old one's favorite boy never did much good when he was alive. I won't grieve for him. Let him stay with Hel where he belongs."

When this news reached Hel, any chance of her releasing Balder was lost. What was worse, this unkind giantess turned out not to be a giantess at all. Thok was none other than Loki in disguise.

Not content with having tricked blind Hoder into killing his twin brother, Loki was denying Balder his life a second time. No wonder that Loki fled to Midgard, the world of humans, to hide from the gods. He built a house on top of a mountain. It had a doorway in each wall, so he could see in all directions and escape if he saw someone coming.

Loki chose a place near a waterfall and spent much of the time disguised as a salmon hiding in the river beneath it.

Soon he began to worry that one day Odin might be sitting on his throne, Hlidskialf, and see him turn into a salmon, thus learning his trick. In those days people caught fish with their hands, a hook, or a spear . . . but Loki remembered the net he'd used to capture Andvari— the one the goddess Ran used to capture drowning sailors. What if one of the gods sent to hunt him down had such a net?

Loki decided to be prepared. He would make his own net, turn himself back into a salmon, and practice escaping from it. That way, if the day came when he was faced with Ran's net, he would know all the tricks. He hurried to his house, found some strong twine, sat down in front of the fire, and began to knot it into a net.

As it happened, that very morning Odin had been sitting on his throne, looking out into the nine worlds, when his eye had been drawn to Midgard and to a strange-looking house . . . with Loki inside.

Odin leaped to his feet and summoned Thor for his strength and Kvasir for his wisdom. Together they would hunt down Loki and put an end to his treachery forever.

As Loki sat in his house working on his net, he saw through an open doorway that the three gods were approaching. The moment he saw them, he threw the half-made net into the fire, then dashed out through a doorway on the other side of the house.

He almost threw himself down the mountain, his feet barely touching the rocky path as he raced to the waterfall. There he dived into the icy water, turning himself into a salmon and hiding behind a rock on the riverbed.

When the three gods entered the house, Loki was long gone, but wise Kvasir strode straight over to the hearth. The fire had been lit some time before, but someone had recently thrown something on it. He stamped out the flames and pulled the object out of the ashes.

"This looks very much like part of the goddess Ran's net," he told the others with a puzzled frown.

"But Ran would never come onto dry land, and she would never light a fire," Odin mused. "How strange."

"Enough of this," snorted Thor impatiently. "Where is Loki?"

"Nearby, I suspect," said Kvasir. "This piece of net was thrown onto the fire only recently, and look. . . ." He bent and picked up the ball of twine. "That's all this ever was, a piece of net, not a whole one."

"What would Loki want with a net?" Thor roared. He didn't want to stand there reasoning; he wanted to find Loki and put an end to him.

"That's it!" said Kvasir, suddenly. "Loki must have been testing his defenses against whatever we throw at him."

"And why would we throw a net at him?" asked Odin.

"Because he's changed himself into a fish!" said Kvasir. "As soon as he saw us coming, he must have gone to the river and changed his shape."

"The scheming shapeshifter!" muttered Thor. So the three gods set about making a fishing net with the twine Loki had left behind.

When the net was finished, the gods made their way down the mountain path, cast the net into the water, and dragged the riverbed. The net didn't quite reach the riverbed, and because Loki stayed low and behind his rock, the net came up empty.

"We must add weights to the bottom of the net," said Kvasir. "That way it will drag the riverbed and force out anyone hiding there!"

So they tied weights to the net and dragged the river a second time. At the last possible moment, Loki jumped out of the water, over the net, and up the waterfall, just as salmon do to this day.

Thor watched. He was sure that the salmon he had seen escape was none other than the slippery Loki. . . . He saw the fish fall back down the waterfall into the river. They would be ready for him next time!

For the third time Kvasir and Odin lowered the net into the water. Foolishly Loki tried using the same trick. When the net came toward him, he gave a huge jump, which carried him out of the water . . . and into the waiting arms of Thor, who caught him just above the tail.

Back in his usual form, Loki was dragged struggling into a cavern deep beneath a mountain.

"Now you will pay for your cruel tricks and the death of my twin sons!" cried Odin, his words echoing around the dark, dank walls. "I have summoned two of your children to join us."

"What do you want with them?" Loki moaned, struggling to free himself from Thor's grip.

"You shall see," said Odin grimly.

Soon two of Loki's children arrived—not Fenris the wolf, not Jormungand the giant serpent, nor Hel the goddess of death —but the two sons Loki had with his wife, the goddess Sigyn.

"They've done you no harm. Let them go!" Loki pleaded.

Odin said nothing, but simply touched the one called Vali. He instantly turned into a wolf and pounced on his brother, Narve, tearing him to shreds before his father's eyes. Odin then pulled out Narve's insides and wove them into a rope, which he, Kvasir, and Thor used to tie the struggling Loki to three huge boulders.

Odin then turned the rope into iron.

"Skadi!" he bellowed into the cavern, and a huge mountain giantess loomed out of the darkness, clutching an enormous serpent.

Without a word the giantess fixed the snake above Loki's head.

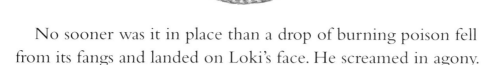

No sooner was it in place than a drop of burning poison fell from its fangs and landed on Loki's face. He screamed in agony.

"Here you will remain until the end of the world," said Odin, and—despite all the terrible things Loki had done—there was a trace of sadness in the voice of the chief of all the gods.

Thor fixed a stare upon him. "Your deeds will live on, Loki," he said. "Tales of your trickery will be told for a thousand years. . . ."

"And all that time you will be here at the mercy of the serpent's venom," Kvasir reminded him.

As the three gods turned to leave Loki, his wife, Sigyn, hurried into the cavern, clutching a large bowl, which she held above her husband's head to catch the poison from the snake's fangs.

Whenever the bowl was full, Sigyn moved it aside to tip the poison on the floor. When, in that brief moment, a drop of poison burned Loki's face, he screamed so loud and writhed in such pain that it echoed under the ground, causing earthquakes.

There Loki remains until Ragnarok—the final battle at the end of the world. Then, according to those who can read the future, Loki will be set free and will rise up with his son, the wolf Fenris, to fight alongside the giants against the gods of Asgard.

# INDEX

First published in the UK in 1997 by

Belitha Press Ltd
London House, Great Eastern Wharf,
Parkgate Road, London SW11 4NQ

Copyright in this format © Belitha Press 1♦
Text copyright © Philip Ardagh 1997
Illustrations copyright © Belitha Press 199♦

Philip Ardagh asserts his moral right to
be identified as the author of this work.

Editor: Mary-Jane Wilkins
Designer: Jamie Asher
Consultant: Liz Bassant

Printed in Hong Kong

Published in the United States in 1999 by

Dillon Press
A Division of Simon & Schuster
299 Jefferson Road
Parsippany, New Jersey 07054-0480

Library of Congress
Cataloging-in-Publication Data

Ardagh, Philip.
Norse myths & legends/as told by Philip
Ardagh: illustrated by Stephen May.
  p. cm.
Includes index.
Contents: Myth or legend?--Gods, giants
& dwarfs--Thor in the land of the giants--
The curse of Andvari's ring--Tyr and the
jaws of Fenris-- The god who loved a gian♦
--Thor's stolen hammer--The trick that ki♦
a god--Balder's fate & Loki's downfall.
Summary: A retelling in a clear, entertainin♦
way of some of the most exciting of the
ancient Norse myths and legends of gods,
giants, dwarfs, dragons, and humans.
1. Mythology, Norse--Juvenile literature.
2. Legends--Scandinavia--Juvenile literatur♦
3. Northmen--Folklore--Juvenile literature♦
[1.Mythology, Norse.] I. May, Stephen, ill.
II. Title.
BL 860.A73 1999
293'.13--dc21                          97-29439
ISBN 0-382-39994-3 (LSB) 10 9 8 7 6 5 4 ♦
ISBN 0-382-39995-1 (PBK) 10 9 8 7 6 5 4 ♦